The Newcomer:
A Saint Maggie Short Story

The Newcomer:
A Saint Maggie Short Story

Janet R. Stafford

Squeaking Pips Books
2020

First Printing:2020

ISBN 978-0-9992285-9-3

Squeaking Pips Books
Hillsborough, NJ 08844

www.squeakingpips.com

Contents

Dedication

To my friends and family, who encourage me to keep writing.

To my parents who instilled in me a love of learning.

To my sister, Diane, and her partner Sarah for being my support.

And to my beta readers, who want to be the first to see what's next for Maggie and her family and who offer me so much helpful, constructive criticism and encouragement.

Preface

When I wrote *Saint Maggie*, the story began in 1860. After all, an author must start somewhere. In that first book we meet Maggie Beatty Blaine, a widow who runs a boarding house. We also meet her boarders, one of whom is Elijah Smith, whom she marries in that first book.

I didn't intend to write a series, but readers of the first novel kept asking me, "What happens next?" As I tried to answer that question and as the series grew, my characters also began revealing their backstories. In addition, I have used short stories to provide background on my characters.

So, now it is Eli's turn. Why did he come to Blaineton and how did he end up living in the little building called the "old caretaker's house"?

I've always believed that kindness brings out the best in most people and can and will result in their being kind to others. Likewise, meanness and cruelty have a similar impact: one person's evil can and will cause an individual to inflict it on someone else. Therefore, if the only thing my books and characters do is inspire a reader to be kind and understanding to another person, then I will feel that they have done their job.

That said, I hope you enjoy this tale about how kindness on Maggie's part helps a weary traveler with a sketchy past finally find a home.

Introduction

If you've never read one of my books before, let me give you a bit of background on the "Saint Maggie universe."

The original story is rooted in research I did while working on my Ph.D. in North American Religion and Culture. I was taking a tutorial on scandals in the Methodist ministry and was required to write a research paper on one. I discovered a tragic story about a talented and charismatic young minister named Jacob Harden. He lived in Warren County, NJ during the 1850s and ended up in a shotgun marriage - the result of his own charisma and some major plotting on the part of his future mother-in-law. Predictably, the marriage was not happy and Harden's response to the miserable situation did not live up to the expectations one might have of a clergyman. (And that is putting it mildly.)

The story stayed with me long after the paper had been graded. A few years after grad school, I found myself wondering how it might be fictionalized into a novel. Eventually, I did write the novel. And, after many years and drafts, I had a character-driven semi-mystery set in the early 1860s. I called it *Saint Maggie*, after the novel's good-hearted, Methodist widow, Maggie Blaine.

I became a self-published author in 2011, and released *Saint Maggie* through my micro-

publishing company, Squeaking Pips Press, Inc.
I have since dissolved Squeaking Pips Press, Inc.
and now operate as Squeaking Pips Books.

Saint Maggie begins when our central
character receives the new minister, Jeremiah
Madison, into her boarding house. This is a last-
resort placement on the part of her church, since
Maggie's other boarders are a group of societal
outcasts: a failed aging writer, an old Irish
immigrant of no fixed job, a broke, struggling
young lawyer, and the undertaker's apprentice.

In addition, I gave Maggie two teenage
daughters: Lydia, the sensible one with a knack
for nursing, and the younger one, outspoken,
opinionated Frances (Frankie for short).

Also living in the house are Emily Johnson,
who does the cooking, and Nate, her carpenter
husband. Emily is Maggie's closest friend but
because the Johnsons are Black and Maggie is
white, their close friendship does not sit well
with the town, especially since the boarding
house is located on the town square.

Finally, we have Elijah Smith. When *Saint
Maggie* begins, Eli is the editor of a penny weekly
called the *Gazette*. A former Quaker and self-
proclaimed free-thinker, Eli is sweet on Maggie,
and she on him. "The Newcomer" sets out to give
us part of Eli's backstory, including the fact that
he has no trouble doing things of a slightly illegal

nature, such as breaking into a house or sneaking into a barn to find shelter for the night.

The story takes us back to 1855. Some of Maggie's boarders are different (for instance, the young lawyer and the undertaker's apprentice arrive years later) and her daughters are still children, twelve and eight years old respectively. But she is still the compassionate woman we meet in *Saint Maggie*, still a woman of faith, and still passionately anti-slavery, as Eli soon will learn.

All that said, I hope you will enjoy the story. I know I enjoyed writing it.

10 March 1855

The locomotive's brakes squealed in complaint as it pulled the train up to the platform.

"Blaineton!" the conductor bellowed. "All off for Blaineton! Blaineton!"

A short, dark-haired man in his mid-thirties hopped to his feet and, standing on his toes, reached into the overhead rack to grab a faded carpet bag. It fell into his arms, one corner grazing his head on the way down.

"Ow!" he squeaked. He took a breath to steady himself, pushed his wire rim glasses back up his nose, shrugged on his coat, and made his way to the car's exit.

Outside the air was chilly, which was as it should be. He was in New Jersey, after all, and it was early March. Overhead, slate gray clouds threatened to discharge their load of snow any minute. As the man looked around, he took note of the piles of slush pushed to the sides of the platform.

Turning to the conductor, he said, "Excuse me. I have a crate in the baggage car." He paused briefly to dig through various pockets until, with a satisfied grunt, he produced a card and handed it to the conductor. "Would it be possible for me to store it here until I'm ready to continue my journey to New York City?"

"Of course, sir." The conductor glanced briefly at the card. "We have a storage room here, Mr. Smith. When you're ready to claim it, please go to the front office, present your ticket, and we will place your property in the appropriate baggage car for you."

The newcomer nodded his thanks and started down the platform toward the street. He wondered if the town had an inn. Then he wondered if he could afford an inn. His first mission therefore was to find a place in which to take shelter for the night. If worse came to worst, he could always sneak into a barn and sleep there. He had done it before. A barn would be warm if animals were present. And even if there were no animals, he always could burrow in the hay.

The little town of Blaineton, New Jersey was comprised of a quaint collection of buildings: some from the pre-Revolutionary era and many from the earlier part of the current century, with a few more up-to-date structures sprinkled throughout for good measure.

The man came to what he figured was the center of town – houses, businesses, a large white church with a tall steeple, and a courthouse – all arranged around a parklike area of trees and field. The snow coated its ground and would have been a pretty sight, had it not been disrupted by all the tracks made by the community's adults, children, and animals.

As the stranger exhaled, his breath turned into a chill, white vapor. It was cold. He was cold.

Blaineton was, from all appearances, a nice little town. Perhaps he could pick up a job or two, earn a bit of money, and move on to his true destination of New York City. And yet he had mixed feelings about returning to the place he had left nearly fifteen years earlier.

No sooner had that thought crossed his mind than he was besieged by every unwanted memory he had stuffed down. There they were: joy and love, heartbreak and depression, success and failure. It made him wonder why he wanted to go back to New York after all. Then again, he had to go somewhere after what had happened in Ohio.

Puffing out another cloud in a sigh, the man turned to his left and strolled down the block, pausing at the very next cross street. After making a quick decision, he turned, walked down it and headed south.

The first house that sat directly on the square turned out to be part of a large parcel that extended to the street behind it, the street on which he now stood. The property had the usual outhouse, a small barn, a woodshed, and a henhouse. The man made a note to return to the barn after dark if he couldn't find an inn to accommodate his miniscule budget.

Then his eyes landed on something interesting: a compact, two-story outbuilding that faced the street he was on. It seemed to be part of the other house's property. Raising a dark eyebrow, the man first checked to make sure he wasn't being observed, and then casually approached the structure.

It looked uninhabited. He went to the least public side of the building and used the sleeve of his coat to rub dirt from one of the windows so he could peer inside.

He saw that the first floor was comprised of a single room. It had a pot belly stove, a table with two – no, three – chairs around it, and a cupboard. At the right side of the room was a door that lead outside. Another door was located at the back of the room. He figured it most likely led to the cellar. The front door, the one that faced the street, was to the room's left. He also saw a stairway leading upstairs that bisected the building, thus creating a tiny parlor close to the front door and narrow hallway between it and the kitchen.

The place looked uninhabited.

Pursing his lips, the man nodded in approval to himself. After taking another quick glance around, he walked to the back door and experimentally turned its knob.

"Locked," he hissed. "Damn!"

"Whatcha doin', mister?" a little voice abruptly piped.

Startled, he turned to find a small girl. She was dressed in a dark blue coat that was way too big for her. A mass of wavy, red hair plotted to escape from under her homemade, knit bonnet. This was tied under her chin in a sloppy, lopsided bow. Her large, green eyes blinked, and she repeated, "Whatcha doin', mister?"

"Um..." he released the knob and lied, "Nothing." Glancing up at the building, he added, "Nice place. Anybody live here?"

"Nope."

"Huh." He considered the house for a moment as an idea dawned on him. "Does that mean it's up for rent?"

The little girl frowned. "I dunno. But you can talk to my Mama. She'll know if we're rentin' it."

"Does she own this place?"

The girl nodded.

"What's your name?"

"Frankie."

"What's Frankie short for?"

She grimaced. "Frances. I hate it." After considering him for a moment, she said, "What's *your* name?"

"Smith."

"You got a first name?"

He grinned. "Mister."

The child laughed. "You're funny!" Then she nodded toward the big house at the other end of the property. "Come on." With a confident gait, she began trudging through the snow.

The man grabbed his carpet bag and followed. "You live in that big house?"

"Yep." Pausing, she turned and met his eyes. "It belongs to my Mama. It's a boarding house. And we have a room open right now." With that, she began walking again, saying to the air, "You can rent that, if you want."

"Actually," the man said, "I'm more interested in that little house back there."

She turned. "That might cost more than a room would, you know."

"Oh, I figured that much." He chuckled, amused that he was dickering about housing with a little gal of – what? – eight, nine years of age?

The child began marching to the house again. Then she led him up some steps to the back door, which she flung open. Looking over her shoulder, she said, "Come on in, Mr. Smith."

The man could smell the delicious aroma of stew and freshly baked bread wafting out of the building. His stomach growled. It was almost noontime and he hadn't eaten since the noon before.

"Sure," he said. "Let's go."

"Mama!" little Frankie bellowed as she traipsed through the door. "*Mama!*"

"Frances Deborah Blaine," a stern voice shot back. "What did your Mama tell you about coming in the kitchen after she just washed the floor? Do you wanna get it all muddy?"

The man cautiously poked his head in the doorway.

A woman with skin the color of hot cocoa was standing at the stove. She was in the process of stirring whatever was in the pot. He figured it was the stew.

Lamb stew, he decided, and his stomach growled again. He hoped no one heard it. He had a good appetite and the belly to prove it.

The woman abruptly turned her head toward him, and Eli momentarily was taken aback by the beauty of her amber eyes.

"Good morning," he said, removing his hat.

She glowered at him. "And just who are *you*?"

"Smith," he stammered. "Elijah Smith. My friends call me Eli. I'm looking for a place to stay."

The woman's suspicion quickly departed, and was replaced by a cordial smile. "Well, how do you, Mr. Smith." She bobbed a brief curtsy in his direction.

He politely bowed back. "How do you do. And you are?"

"Mrs. Johnson. Emily Johnson." She returned her attention to the pot, removed the big wooden spoon from it and set it on a plate.

"Pleased to meet you, Mrs. Johnson."

Frankie piped up, "Mr. Smith wants to rent a room."

7

"Mm, hm," Emily replied. "That's the man said. Well, you know what to do, honey. Go get your Mama."

The child scampered off

"Would you care to have dinner with us, Mr. Smith?" Emily asked.

Would he? His mouth was watering like mad. "I'd like that very much, Mrs. Johnson. What do you charge here for a meal?"

She smiled. "Nothing."

He blinked in surprise. "Nothing?"

"That's right. You'll be our guest today. Mind you, it's simple fair – stew, bread, butter, fried apples. And of course, coffee. But you're welcome to it."

He hadn't encountered such open hospitality since he had sojourned with the Sioux. But that wasn't entirely true, he reminded himself. He had experienced kindness from people with dark and light skin alike during his journey.

The trip from Ohio through Pennsylvania to New Jersey had been a rigorous onw. He had taken a train as far as he could in Ohio, disembarked, and had worked any kind of job he could find, sleeping usually in barns or other outbuildings. His mealtime had consisted of eating either standing up or sitting in a pile of straw or even on the ground. Once he had earned enough money in one location, he would take another train to another place and repeat the process. He was tired and welcomed the opportunity to sit a table like a human being.

"I would be happy to be your guest, Mrs. Johnson," Eli replied, meaning every word.

Frankie's little voice came from the hallway. "He's in here, Mama!"

The child strode back into the kitchen, holding the hand of a slender woman with skin as pale as her daughter's, although unfreckled. Her eyes were wide and hazel in color. And she had auburn hair, from what Eli could see of the few strands peeking out from beneath the kerchief she wore on her head. Her face was rather plain, but pleasant to look at. Her dress, a worn affair of faded blue, was covered by a patched, pink gingham apron.

So, that's Mama, he thought.

Although he knew full well that the woman was not technically a beauty (she was too thin and tired-looking for that), Eli still found her attractive. There was something about her, an aura that bespoke kindness and generosity before she even had uttered a word.

"Mr. Smith?" she said, in a pleasant voice somewhere in the alto range.

"Yes," he said. "Elijah Smith."

"His friends call him Eli," Emily commented with a droll smile as she went back to stirring the stew.

After casting an affectionate smile at Emily, the other woman returned her eyes to Eli. "I'm

Mrs. Blaine. Maggie Blaine. I understand you wish to rent a room."

"Yes." He hesitated and then decided to press on. "Could we speak privately, Mrs. Blaine?"

The woman glanced at her friend. "There's nothing you can say to me that cannot be said in front of Mrs. Johnson."

He saw Emily Johnson throw a side glance his way. He quickly amended, "I surmised as much, but you see, I've had a long journey, Mrs. Blaine, and I'm bone-weary and I have some questions and..."

She smiled again. "I understand. Leave your bag here and we'll go to the parlor. Follow me, please."

Frankie tailed them on their way out of the kitchen until Maggie turned and said quietly to her daughter, "There's no need for you to come with us, dear. I'm afraid the conversation will take a rather dull turn from now on."

Frankie uttered a disappointed, "aww," but retreated obediently into the kitchen.

"I'm sorry if she bothered you, Mr. Smith," Maggie commented as they continued down a hall. "Frankie can be quite a precocious child."

"Actually, she's quite a delightful child," he replied. "We had an interesting conversation outside. She's the one who told me that you run a boarding house."

"Oh, she does that all the time! She fills our rooms better than our sign out front does."

Maggie paused in front of what he presumed was the formal parlor. "Here we are. Do come in, Mr. Smith and have a seat."

"Thank you." Eli found a comfortable chair and sank onto it.

Maggie seated herself nearby. "I apologize for my appearance, but I have been engaged in housekeeping. You see, Mrs. Johnson and I are the only ones who keep the house and fix the meals."

"So, Mrs. Johnson is in your employ?"

"Well, one *might* say that. It started out that way, but over the course of three years, she has become my friend. Mrs. Johnson and her husband, and my daughters and I live in the new wing. Our boarders live here in the old building. Their bed chambers are upstairs."

Maggie Blaine did not speak like an uneducated woman. In fact, Eli thought, if he was any judge of language, she spoke like someone of means. He wondered what had happened to put her in this situation.

"The room we have to let is quite comfortable and it faces the square and catches the morning sun. It's airy and bright, and I assure you spotlessly clean. I know you will like it very much."

"Actually," Eli cut in, "I was thinking about that little place at the end of the property."

Maggie's large eyes grew larger yet. "You mean the old caretaker's house? Oh, but Mr.

Smith, no one's lived there for years. It surely wants a thorough cleaning and the roof must leak and the windows, too!"

"It'll be fine," he assured her.

"But it would be so much work for you. You'd be much happier here up in that lovely room. Really."

He wondered why she was backing away from a chance to rent an entire building, even if he hadn't figured out yet how to pay for the first few months. She almost appeared to be nervous about renting the place.

"It's no trouble," Eli replied. "I'm used to living in less than, shall we say, ideal circumstances."

"But..." She faded off.

"What?" Now he was curious, which was bad news for her. He was a natural-born truth-ferret.

"Well, it's just sometimes the building is used for *other* purposes."

"I thought you said it hadn't been used in years."

Maggie looked away from his gaze to stare at the wall behind him. "Yes. I suppose I had."

"Then what do you do in it? Raising chickens?"

"Of course not!"

"Pigs?"

She smiled faintly. "Now you're being absurd."

"Then what? Why are you hesitating to rent it? Is it haunted or something?"

"No!" Maggie momentarily twisted her hands, but quickly composed herself and took a breath. "Well, I suppose it wouldn't hurt to show it to you. But you'll see how much work it needs. And you haven't told me yet why you require all that space."

Eli nodded. "Fair enough. Mrs. Blaine, I'm a newspaperman. Back in Ohio, I printed a weekly paper called *The Bugle*. But now I'm on my way back to New York City to see if I can find work at one of the papers there."

He paused long enough for her to say, "What happened to your newspaper in Ohio?"

"Ah, well, I wrote some editorials that certain people took offense at and next thing I knew the sheriff turned up at my door. He told me some folks thought I'd look a whole lot better at the end of a rope and that I needed to get out of town. Quick."

"Good heavens!" she gasped. "You don't mean to say they wanted to hang you?"

"Yep. Anyway, I managed to throw my clothes in my carpetbag, grab my case full of type and leading, and hop onto the sheriff's wagon. He got me out of town before the rowdies arrived at my place. Good timing if there ever was such a thing, huh? But, when the rowdies didn't find me, they burned everything down, printing press and all. Guess it made 'em feel better, especially since they were deprived of stringing me up."

Maggie leaned toward him. "Whatever did you write to make them so angry?"

He hesitated, then said, "It was an editorial about abolition. Mrs. Blaine, I'm anti-slavery, and that pack of madmen weren't."

He did not expect what happened next.

Maggie's eyes lit up like a chandelier in a ballroom. "You're anti-slavery? So am I! Have you ever read *The National Era*[1]?

Eli chuckled. "Never miss an issue." Then he added, "Well, not until two months ago, that is."

"I'm so sorry to hear what happened to you." He could tell by her tone that she meant it.

"Thank you. But I've become adept at landing on my feet. Anywaywhen I saw the caretaker's building on your property, I suddenly thought it would be a dandy spot to start another paper."

"Oh, I'm so glad you changed your plans. That old house would serve you very well." Enthused, Maggie added, "And you may live here in the room upstairs until you have the other place ready."

She was such a nice woman. Eli suffered a momentary pang of guilt. Then he heaved a sigh. He needed to tell her something. "Mrs. Blaine," he began, "there's one other thing I neglected to tell you."

---

[1] *The National Era* was a well-known abolitionist publication published in Washington, DC from 1847-1860. It ran Harriet Beecher Stowe's novel, *Uncle Tom's Cabin* as a serial in 1851.

"Tell me, please."

"I don't have any money. I mean, I *do*, but it's only fifty cents. I'll gladly give it all to you, if you'll just give me the time to repair the house, set up my press, and get a few issues out."

A frown lightly creased her forehead.

"Look, I have my typeface and leading stored over at the depot. I don't have the vaguest idea how to build a flatbed press, but I'll do it somehow. You have my word."

Maggie still said nothing.

"And," he hurriedly added, "I'll do anything else you need. I'm good at, you know, all sorts of stuff."

She held up her hand. "Mr. Smith. Stop. Please."

He did, as flop sweat broke out on the back of his neck and under his arms. She was going to send him packing. He just knew it.

And then Maggie smiled. "You may have the house."

"I may?" He scarcely could believe his ears.

"Mr. Smith, what kind of Christian would I be if I didn't help my fellow man?"

"Thank you." Then he grinned. "So, tell me. What kind of Christian *are* you, Mrs. Blaine?"

"A Methodist. What kind are you?"

"Oh." He played for time. Should he tell her? What would she think of him? Oh, who cared, anyway? He forged on, "I was raised in the Society of Friends."

"So, you're a Quaker."

"Was," he corrected. "I'm, uh, not really connected to a Meeting anymore."

"Oh, I'm sorry to hear that. Faith is important."

Now he was worried again. "But I *have* faith, Mrs. Smith. I just don't practice it with a Meeting. I hope that won't change anything about my staying here."

With a slight smile, Maggie shook her head. "No. If my Savior didn't discriminate then why should I? All are welcome here." Her smile now became a bit playful. "Besides, I think Blaineton could use a newspaper."

His jaw nearly hit the floor. "You don't have one yet? Even a penny weekly?"

"No! And I think we should have one. We may be small town, but, Mr. Smith, things happen here – elections, summer and harvest fairs, fetes, church picnics, even trials. A weekly paper would be a fine thing."

Impulsively, Eli stood up, strode over and took her hands in his. "Mrs. Blaine, I solemnly promise that I will pay back every single penny I owe and more."

Maggie rose so that they now stood face to face. "It is a deal, sir."

Her announcement was followed by an awkward pause, which lasted until Eli realized that he was still holding her hands.

"Oh!" He immediately let go. "I'm sorry," he stammered, stepping back to put more space between them. "I mean, that's splendid."

Maggie blushed and looked down at her feet.

Eli cleared his throat. "May we take a look at the building now?"

She chuckled. "By all means. I have the key on my ring. Let's go."

"Perfect!" Eli announced as he and Maggie entered the house's first floor. "There's enough room for a flatbed press. That table can be my desk. I'll use the cupboard for supplies. And that stove'll come in handy next winter."

"There's another little stove upstairs," Maggie told him. "I'm afraid neither one is large enough to do anything other than fry an egg or boil coffee. I encourage you to take your meals with the other boarders. Your rent will cover that."

But Eli had thrown open the doors to the cupboard and was busy surveying its interior. He heard Maggie say something but did not catch what it was.

"Beg pardon?"

"You'll be eating with us, I hope," she repeated with a smile.

"Oh! Yeah." He shut the cupboard doors and turned to face his new landlady. "I'm a terrible cook."

"I'm glad. I mean, not because you're a terrible cook, but because that way you'll be able to get to know a few people." Maggie gestured at the cupboard. "So, do you think you'll be able use that for your paper and other supplies?"

He nodded. "It'll do fine. More than fine! May I see the upstairs room now?"

The second floor contained a bed and bedside table, a wardrobe, and a chest of drawers. Eli thought the wardrobe could always do double duty and hold additional supplies if, by some strange chance, his newspaper started to boom.

He heard Maggie say, "Of course, this room wants a good airing out and a coat of paint. I'll ask Nate Johnson to check the roof and windows for leaks."

"Thanks." Eli sat tentatively on the bed to test it out.

It promptly sank.

He flailed wildly, to no avail, to stop his disappearing into the mattress. Fortunately, Maggie hurried to his side and held her hands out. He grasped them like a drowning man.

"Hold still," he told her. "Let me get my footing and pull myself up."

Maggie braced herself. She was strong, having done her share of manual labor, and it took but a second for Eli to get out of his predicament and stand beside her once again.

She giggled in amusement. "I daresay the bedframe's ropes need a great deal tightening!"

"I think the mattress needs to be stuffed, too, while we're at it," Eli added, with a grin.

Maggie released his hands. "I warned you that this place needed fixing up."

"And fix it up, we shall!"

The two returned to the narrow flight of stairs and descended to the first floor.

Eli gestured at the extra door in the kitchen. "That leads to the cellar, right?"

"It does. However, I must insist that you refrain from going down there."

Eli's dark brows arched upward. "Why? What's down there? Skeletons?"

She laughed.

He thought it was a pretty sound.

"Heavens, no," she said. "We have nothing to hide. It's just we use it for storage. Also, the steps are rather in need of repair, and I would hate to see you fall through."

"Fair enough."

But Eli's newspaperman instincts were alerting him to a story the way a hound alerts to a scent.

"Now..." Maggie indicated the little house's back door. "Allow me to show you to your *temporary* quarters.

###

The room in the boarding house was exactly as Maggie claimed it would be - comfortable, full of light, and airy. Eli set his carpet bag on the bed and, before unpacking, took a moment to gaze out the window at the square. Once spring got fully underway, he realized, the view would be lovely.

Maggie left to help Emily with the noon dinner, and, for the next half hour, Eli busied himself with putting away his few clothes and other items. He even tested the mattress on the bed, found it to be quite comfortable, and stretched out on it.

When he heard the dinner bell ring, he went down to the formal dining room, the place where Maggie had told him the noon meal would be held.

He was the first one there. As he stepped into the room, Eli took in the starched, white tablecloth, the silverware, the old, well-used china, and the water glasses, some of which had a chip or two in them.

As he strolled along the table toward a likely seat, he noticed a mended spot on the tablecloth. Eli smiled to himself. He was dealing with thrifty and humble people.

Well, good. He liked thrifty and humble people. There were far too many strutting, self-important bullies loose in the world.

Footsteps on the hallway's wood floor told him that other boarders were arriving. Eli took a seat and waited.

The first one to enter was a white-haired gentleman with a dapper moustache. He sat beside Eli and smiled welcomingly, blue eyes crinkling at their corners.

"You must be the new boarder," he said. "I'm Chester Carson."

He offered Eli his hand. Eli took it and they shook.

"Pleased to meet you, Mr. Carson. I'm Eli Smith."

"My pleasure, Mr. Smith."

The others in the household came in shortly: James O'Reilly, a thin, old Irishman; and Arthur Graham, a young man of no more than 20 years. Then there was Nathaniel Johnson, Emily's husband. He was a man around 30 years of age and was possessed of dark brown skin, black eyes, and short cropped hair.

Finally, little Frankie stomped in. She plopped down onto her seat and wiped her nose on the back of her hand

She was followed by a taller girl, who appeared to be about twelve or thirteen years of age. And she was chiding her little sister.

"Oh, honestly. Do use your hankie, Frances!"

This girl's hair was brown, as were her eyes. Yet Eli still could see her resemblance to Frankie and Maggie.

That's got to be Maggie's other daughter, he thought. Then he wondered if any more children were about to appear.

As the others at table chattered among themselves, Mr. Carson leaned over to Eli. "Those are Mrs. Blaine's children. The youngest is Frankie. The eldest is Lydia."

So, there were only two and both girls.

"I've met Frankie," Eli said as he watched the two sisters.

Lydia currently was engaged in pushing Frankie's elbows off the table.

"She's quite a character, isn't she?"

"Oh, she is indeed," the other man replied. "A bit of a hoyden, yet one can't help but love her. Mrs. Blaine has her hands full, to be sure, especially since she is a widow."

For some reason, this took Eli aback. He had assumed that since Maggie was a "Mrs." there was a Mr. Blaine somewhere.

"I'm sorry to hear that," he murmured. "A woman as nice as she is ought to be married."

Mr. Carson took his napkin out of its ring and placed it upon his lap. "I agree. The poor fellow died of rheumatic fever in '50. So did their little boy."

At this news, Eli felt a familiar pang in his heart. He hated loss, whether it was his own or someone else's. Sometimes it felt as if he had experienced nothing but loss throughout his life. The bad times were interspersed with good times, to be sure, but the difficulties left an indelible mark.

He wondered if that was how it was with everyone. And did the pain and sadness ever go away?

He sighed inwardly. *Enough thinking about that.*

Fortunately, he was distracted by Maggie and Emily's arrival. Emily was bearing a tureen of stew. This she placed at the head of the table and then hurried out again. Maggie, meanwhile, set a bowl of butter and a plate piled high with hearty slices of bread in the middle of the table. As Maggie went to take her place at the head, Emily returned with a steaming pot of coffee.

It all smelled so very good. Eli scarcely could wait.

Maggie said, "Mr. Johnson, would you do us the honor of saying grace?"

"I'd be happy to, Mrs. Blaine." Nate turned to the others. "Everybody, please bow."

All heads looked down at hands folded on the tabletop.

Eli surreptitiously peeked up to watch Nate. The man had large, calloused hands – powerful hands. Maggie said he was a carpenter, which made Eli wonder if Nate knew how to build a flatbed press.

"Our Father," the carpenter intoned, "bless this food and bless the hands that prepared it. May it fill us to go out and do thy will the rest of this day. Amen."

"Amen," everyone chimed.

Finally, it was time to eat!

Eli happily received his bowl of stew, took two pieces of bread, liberally buttered them, and dug in. Everything was delicious and filling. When the coffee pot came his way, he poured himself a cup and added to it cream and two lumps of sugar. His first sip made him feel as if he might pass out from joy. The brew was strong and flavorful, just the way he liked it.

Later, they sat over more cups of coffee and a dessert of fried apples with cream.

Eli heaved a contented sigh. "Mrs. Johnson, I have to say that was the best meal I've had in a long time."

Emily smiled. "Why, thank you, Mr. Smith."

Young Arthur Graham asked, "What brought you here, Mr. Smith?"

"Oh, a train," Eli joked.

Everyone laughed.

When they had settled down, he continued, "Truthfully, my plan was to return to New York City after a sojourn in Ohio and the Sioux Territory."

"Sioux Territory," Nate commented. "That's quite a trip."

Eli nodded.

Frankie piped up, "Did you live with Indians, Mr. Smith?"

"I did indeed," he replied.

The child was enthralled. "What were they like?"

24

Eli sat back in his chair. "Oh, very much like you and me, Frankie – only they do things a little differently." He grinned. "Actually, sometimes they do things a *lot* differently. But despite that, they're people who have needs, hopes, fears, and feelings just like we do."

"I'd like to meet them some day," she said.

"Well, maybe you will. Someday."

"But not too soon," Maggie put in.

"Aww, you always say that, Mama," Frankie muttered and shoveled a forkful of fried apples into her mouth.

###

Eli caught up with Nate as he was on his way out of the boarding house. "Mr. Johnson!"

Nate turned. "Why, Mr. Smith! Where are you off to?"

"The train station." Eli found himself a bit puffy. He'd had to canter to catch up with the other man. "I left my letter case in storage at the depot."

"Letter case? As in printing?"

Eli nodded. "I intend to start a newspaper in your fair town, Mr. Johnson."

Nate considered the idea. "Huh. Well, I reckon we could use one."

"That's what Mrs. Blaine said." He glanced at the other man, curious as to what Johnson would say in response to his next comment. "I'm renting the caretaker's house."

Nate stopped walking and turned to face the short newcomer. "Thought you were living in the room we had open in the boarding house."

"I am. Temporarily. But I plan to move to the caretaker's house. I'll live on the second floor and use the first floor as my print shop."

The other man pursed his lips in thought. "Huh." Then he added, "And Mrs. Blaine approved it?"

"Oh, sure." Eli chuckled. "I mean, she had to, since she's the one renting it to me. Right?"

"Huh," Nate repeated, thoughtfully.

Eli studied the dark man's expression. "Something wrong?"

"She told you about the cellar, didn't she?"

"As in I'm not supposed to go down there?"

"Yes, sir."

"She said something about it being used for storage."

Nate replied, "That's right. We keep things down there."

"Oh, yeah? What kind of things?"

"I don't think you'd be interested in them." Nate resumed walking. "Just a bunch of old stuff."

Eli called up a friendly smile and hurried to keep up with him. "They're that boring, huh?"

"Yep. Put you right to sleep."

He's covering something up, Eli thought. *What the hell is down there?*

The two men chatted about other subjects as they continued their journey. Eventually, Eli managed to turn the conversation around to abolition and informed Nate of the reason he had left Ohio in such a hurry.

Nate said, "Folks get all fired up when someone speaks favorably about anti-slavery, don't they?"

"Do you think I'll run into trouble like that here?"

Nate blew out a thoughtful breath. "Well, Mr. Smith, New Jersey does have a fair number of folks who think abolitionists are nothing but troublemakers."

"Hmm."

"And Mrs. Blaine gets her share of snubbing these days."

Eli feigned ignorance. "Is she anti-slavery?"

Nate grinned and nudged him. "Are feathers on a chicken? Sir, Mrs. Blaine has a big heart, a heart big enough to love folks no matter what their color is. She takes Jesus at his word: love others. Of course, there're some around here that don't take kindly to that attitude when it applies to loving folk of another color. But Mrs. Blaine, she stands her ground and tells them slavery's a sin."

"She's telling the truth. And the truth can make people angry." Eli glanced up at Nate. "But

I agree with her. For instance, you and me? The way I see it, we're equal in every way. Except I get opportunities, and you get denied them."

Nate gave him a smile. "You know, I think I like you."

"Do you like me enough to build a flatbed press for me?"

Nate's response was a whistle. "That's a big order."

"I need a simple one, just big enough for a penny weekly paper. I could get the plans and pay you for your work." Even as he said it, Eli was wondering *how* he was going to raise enough cash to purchase the plans, never mind pay for the press itself.

Nate considered his offer. "If you show me the plans, I'll see what I can do."

After Eli arranged to have his case of letters and leading sent to the boarding house, he returned and entered his new home with the key that Maggie had given him.

Pleased, he surveyed the first floor with a sense of satisfaction and anticipation. As his eyes swept over the little room, they landed on the door to the cellar. After the briefest of pauses, he walked slowly over, took hold of the knob, and twisted.

It barely moved.

"Locked" he muttered. "Damn!"

Eli fished the house key out of his jacket pocket and tried it in the keyhole.

It didn't fit.

He removed the key and shoved it back into his pocket.

Obviously, Maggie did not want him, or anyone else for that matter, to go down there.

It was then that it dawned on him. His new landlady had correctly read his curiosity about the cellar. She knew he would try the door.

And she was right.

In truth, he really *wasn't* to be trusted. But that was only because he simply could not resist a mystery.

Never mind, he told himself. *I've got other fish to fry.*

What was behind the door could wait because what couldn't wait was getting a job and some money.

Chapter 2: 17 April 1855

It took Eli over a month to raise the funds to finish paying Nate for the supplies and work he had done while building the flatbed press. All during that time the mystery of the locked cellar door retreated to the back of Eli's mind. He had other things to do and think about.

He quickly found employment in the form of two jobs. One was working in the train station's storage room. The other was at the livery stable cleaning the horses' stalls and seeing to their feed and water.

During the month, he also put in the work needed to make the Old Caretaker's House habitable. Maggie graciously told him that doing repairs to the building would take the place of his rent.

The result of it all was that Eli was busy from sunup to well beyond sundown. Fortunately, even though he was a portly man, he was strong and had stamina. By the end of the day, he fell, completely exhausted, onto his bed at the boarding house and slept soundly until the next morning.

But it was all worth it, for suddenly he found himself at the end of his work. Or more accurately, at the end of *that* kind of work. Getting his newspaper up and running would be his next task.

As Eli looked around the building, he felt a rush of energy and excitement. He was going to have a newspaper again. Finally!

Oh, he knew that as soon as he published his first issue, he would need to hit the streets and sell the paper to whomever he met. That would be a taxing activity, too, as would chasing down and writing up stories of interest. But it would be worth it, all of it. Journalism was his love, and he was a newspaperman through and through. In fact, he strongly suspected that if he pricked his finger, it would bleed ink rather than blood.

Encouraged, Eli left the boarding house, marched to the livery stable, and announced that he regrettably would be resigning. However, he did not do the same with his job at the depot. He realized that he would need a source of income for a few more months at least.

He then walked victoriously to the Second Street Boarding House, enjoyed the usual delicious noon dinner, and proclaimed to one and all that this was the day he would be moving into the caretaker's house, which, he hoped, soon would become known as a print shop.

As he was throwing his meager belongings into his carpet bag, Maggie Blaine appeared in the doorway to his room.

Eli grinned up at her. "I'll be out of here in another minute, Mrs. Blaine. Then you may look for another boarder for this room. One that, I hope, will pay you."

"Oh," she replied, "I'm not bothered by that. Besides what you did for the caretaker's place was worth more than many months' rent."

Impressed by her generous spirit, he stopped working and turned to face her. "You're an astounding woman, Maggie Blaine." Then he chuckled, adding, "But you're a *terrible* businesswoman."

She smiled. "I'm not sure whether to be honored or insulted by that."

"Be honored." Eli closed his carpet bag. "Well, I'll be on my way."

"I'll miss you," she said. She was smiling, but the smile was a bit sad.

He laughed. "Don't worry. I'll be taking all my meals here and probably will join the household in the parlor or out on the porch in the evenings – when I have the time, that is."

"Oh, I hope you do have the time. Otherwise, those evening chats just won't be the same."

Her words touched him. She was saying that he was valued and needed. He had something to offer and was part of the boarding house now, whether he lived there or not. He liked that about Maggie. She had a heart. A big one.

"Thank you," he replied. "I'll try to make the time. I promise."

And he was off.

Eli's first night in his new home filled him with optimism. So much so, that he sat down at the old table in the first floor's room and, opening a notebook, began sketching out ideas for news articles. When the sun set and the room grew chill and dim, he started a fire in the stove and lit the lamp on the table.

He was so absorbed in his work that he lost track of time, only coming to himself when he heard footsteps and the faint murmur of voices outside. They sounded as if they were coming from the street in front of the boarding house.

Frowning, he removed his wire rim glasses, rubbed his eyes, and wondered what time it was. After taking a battered old watch from his waistcoat pocket, Eli blinked at the face until it came into focus.

"Ten thirty," he muttered. What were people doing running around outside at that late hour?

Shrugging the question off, Eli returned to his notebook and worked until his ears caught the sound of more voices. This time, though, they were coming from... where?

He paused and listened.

It didn't sound like they were outside.

So, where were they?

He frowned.

Then he said aloud, "The cellar?"

The mystery of what lay behind the locked door suddenly popped back into his consciousness.

People were in the cellar! His cellar.

But the only entrance Eli knew of was from this room.

How could that be? How could people be in the cellar?

Eli sprang to his feet. But before he could take a step, he was interrupted by knocking on his front door.

"Mr. Smith," a voice urgently whispered. "Mr. Smith, it's Maggie Blaine! Open the door, please! Hurry!"

Confused, he strode over, threw back the bolt, ad opened the door to let her in.

As she rushed past him, Eli shut the door and bolted it. When he turned to face her, he found Maggie, keys in hand, striding toward the cellar.

"What's going on?" he asked.

She stopped at the cellar's door and began sorting through the keys. "Oh, Mr. Smith, I prayed this wouldn't happen."

"What?"

"Put out the light, first. Please."

Eli turned to the lamp on the kitchen table and did as requested.

Maggie found the appropriate key, thrust it into the keyhole, and opened the door.

"Up here!" she called quietly. "Hurry!"

In the next second, two young men of color, both wearing ragged clothing and one holding a lantern, entered the kitchen.

"Mrs. Blaine, what on earth is going on?" Eli repeated.

Maggie blinked at him. "My dear Mr. Smith, considering your support of abolition, surely you must *know* what's going on."

Eli stared at the two men standing by the potbelly stove. And suddenly it was all too clear. But he had one more important question. "How did these men get in my cellar?"

Maggie took a breath. "Back when my Aunt Lettie's family owned this property, they built a tunnel leading from the caretaker's house to the main house. It was used during inclement or snowy weather."

"And now you use it when slave catchers show up uninvited."

"That's right," Maggie concluded hurriedly. She turned to the man with the lantern. "Tom, would you please put out that lamp?"

Tom nodded and in a second the room was in darkness.

"Mr. Smith, please take these men upstairs to the bedroom. I must lock the cellar door. I'll be up shortly. Once you're in the bedroom, you'll need to move the wardrobe. There's a door hidden behind it. Don't light a lamp or you'll give us away."

It was all too familiar to Eli. He remembered well the scurrying about his family did when slave catchers showed up on their property.

He gestured absently to the men and said, "Follow me, gentlemen. Watch your step on the stairs. It's pretty dark in here."

"We don't mind, sir," Jim, the other man, replied. "We're used to getting around without a light."

Once they were upstairs, Eli opened the door to the bedroom and led the men in. The three surveyed the room – it was bathed with faint moonlight coming through the window. Spotting the wardrobe, they went directly to it.

Eli hurried over to help them push the furniture aside. Sure enough, once it had been moved, he saw the secret door in the wall. It was about three feet high. He wondered how much room the hiding place had.

His thoughts were interrupted by the sound of light footsteps on the stairs.

Maggie rushed into the room and turned to Tom and Jim. "They're outside boarding house. You'd best get inside."

Without a word, the two dropped down and crawled into the opening.

Maggie leaned over to speak through the doorway. "I know it is close in there and dark, as well, but please be still until I tell you otherwise."

"Yes, ma'am," Tom said. "Don't worry. We've been in lots of tight spots."

"I imagine you have." Maggie stood up, shut the door, and turned to Eli. "You must not say anything about this to anybody."

He grinned. "I wouldn't worry, Mrs. Blaine. My family not only were Quakers but were station masters on the Underground Railroad line."

She exhaled with relief. "Then you understand."

"Of course. Tell me about your work."

"Emily and Nate are the station masters for this stop. I had suspected such for some time. Recently, though, they took me into their confidence and allowed me to help with their work. My boarders all support and know about our activity. We make sure all newcomers to our home are sympathetic, since it is safer for us and our guests if they are. Sometimes it's difficult to hide what we are doing, as you well know."

She brushed stray wisps of hair back from her face. Eli noticed that her hair was in a braid. She must have dressed quickly. Perhaps she had gone to bed fully clothed in anticipation of the slave catchers.

She nodded at the closed door in the wall. "Shall we move the wardrobe back into place?"

No longer had they done that, than they heard voices nearby.

"Oh, dear," Maggie whispered in a panic. "They're right outside! Shut the bedroom door, Mr. Smith. Quickly!"

Eli did as he was told. "How do you figure the slave catchers suspected your house?"

"Rumors," she replied. "I am friends with the people of color who live up on Water Street and, well, I'm also outspoken about my feelings on slavery. One of the Water Street contacts rode down and alerted us about the slave catchers. Like I said, my sympathies are well known throughout the town, so I'm sure some of the copperheads hear have mentioned us to the slave catchers. They would love to see us given a fine we could not pay and therefore thrown into jail." She smiled proudly. "But no one has ever caught us." She peeked out the window. "Good! Mr.

Carson is with them. He'll try to keep them away."

Unfortunately, the voices outside abruptly became argumentative and angry.

"Regardless, of what you claim, you cannot simply burst in there," Mr. Carson boomed. "This is private property!"

"Then go get the sheriff," a male growled. "By the time you get back, we'll have searched the place."

"I must object to this, sir!"

"Get outta our way," another man snapped. "We know those two darkies are here somewhere."

"We don't know what you're talking about." Emily's voice was firm and unafraid. "You can't search that home. One of our boarders lives there!"

"We can do what we want," the first man replied. "Say, where're you from, anyway? You ain't one'a them, are you? If y'are, we could take you back and forget about all this."

Mr. Carson snapped, "Leave her alone! Does she speak as if she had been a slave? As if she had lived in the South?"

"I'll run for the sheriff, Mr. Carson." It was Edgar Lape's voice.

"Thank you," Mr. Carson replied. "Bring him immediately."

The front door clicked open.

"I should go down there," Eli whispered. He could tell Maggie was nervous as a cat. "Maybe I can stop them from going further."

But she shook her head. "They're sure to come up here no matter what you do. Then they'll find me. And when they do, they'll search the room."

They could hear the men checking the first floor.

"We must do something," Maggie murmured, eyes wide. "Oh, Mr. Smith, I don't know what to do."

After a moment's thought, Eli said, "We'll distract them, that's what."

And, without warning, he put an arm around her waist and pulled her close. His hand could feel the armor of her corset, and the barrier her skirt and two petticoats between their bodies. He hadn't been this close to a woman in years.

"Mr. Smith," she hissed, putting her hands against his chest as she tried to push him away. "What in heaven's name are you doing?"

Her indignant scowl was almost amusing.

"Calm down," he replied. "We're going to create a distraction."

"A distraction? *Like this*?"

"Yes! Like this. Now, please, don't take this personally, Mrs. Blaine."

41

Footsteps sounded at the bottom of the stairs.

"Take *what* personally?" Maggie was thoroughly confused, as well as frightened.

"*This!*" Eli wrapped his other arm around her and planted a kiss firmly on her lips.

She broke away, squeaking in protest. "*Mr. Smith!*"

"Shh!" With a touch of agitation in his voice, he added in a hurried whisper, "When they come in the door, they'll see us kissing. And when they see us kissing, they'll forget about searching the room."

The light finally went on in Maggie's head. This time, she did not protest when he kissed her. In fact, she snaked her arms around his neck for good measure.

The bed chamber door banged open.

"What the hell?" a man gasped in surprise.

"Maggie?" a shocked Emily exclaimed.

"Well, lookee that," another fellow commented.

At this, the couple broke their kiss.

As if it were the most natural thing in the world, Eli said, "I don't know what you want, but you picked one hell of a time to show up. Can't a man and his lady have a little privacy?"

The men – three rough-looking characters – immediately backed clumsily out of the room amid a chorus of:

"Sorry!"

"'S'cuse us."

"Beggin' yer pardon."

Then the slave catchers hurriedly retreated down the stairs with Mr. Carson nipping at their heels and chastising them all the way down.

"There! Are you satisfied now? I suppose you'll go chattering about what you saw, thereby ruining my dear landlady's reputation."

In another second they were gone, slamming the front door behind them.

Maggie and Eli simultaneously blew out relieved sighs, disengaged from their embrace, and turned to face Emily who, glowering and arms akimbo, was standing in the doorway. "Margaret Blaine! I never in all my born days would take you for a –"

"For a what?" Eli cut in with a cheeky grin. "For a woman who goes to great lengths to protect people?"

Emily continued to frown. "I hope that's all that was."

Eli chuckled. "Really? Am I such a terrible man as all that?"

"No, sir. Not at all. But you're new here. We don't know you yet. It just seems a bit – too familiar too soon."

At this, Maggie burst into laughter. "Oh, Emily! Sometimes we have to do things we normally would not do in order to save a life."

"Mm, hm," Emily replied skeptically.

"Oh, do stop that! And go on home. Please. I'm fine. I shall return shortly. Mr. Smith and I just need to have a chat first."

"I'm not going anywhere until you get yourself out of this bedroom and downstairs."

Maggie laughed once more. "Fine, we'll go downstairs. But let's get our friends out of the hidey-hole first, and you can escort them back into the cellar."

After Emily and the freedom seekers were gone, Eli invited Maggie to sit at his table while he made a pot of tea. He wondered what she needed to say but decided it was best to let her take her time. He just hoped she wasn't going to kick him out on his backside.

His fears abated as the two chatted amiably over cups of tea laced with milk and sugar.

Finally, Eli decided that it was time to get down to brass tacks. "Mrs. Blaine, allow me to apologize for what happened upstairs."

"Don't," was her surprising reply. "What you did – what *we* did chased the slave hunters away."

He couldn't help it. He grinned now. "Worked pretty well, didn't it?"

"Indeed, it did." Maggie returned the grin and took a sip of tea. As she replaced her cup on the saucer, she said, "I daresay, Mr. Smith, that you're now part of our little operation."

"Thank you. I'm honored."

"I'm sure Mr. and Mrs. Johnson will approve." She chuckled. "At least, once Mrs. Johnson gets over the shock."

Eli smiled, looked down at his tea, and gave it a stir with his spoon. Truth be told, he had liked the kiss. He hadn't kissed a woman in a long time. But he tossed any further ideas aside as he lifted the cup to his lips.

There was a brief silence on both their parts, during which Eli noticed how quiet Blaineton was at night. It was quite nice. He realized that he liked the silence.

"Mr. Smith," Maggie suddenly said.

He looked up.

"I would like us to be friends."

"Thank you. I'd like us to be friends, too." He laughed, "Especially since... you know."

"Yes, especially since... what happened upstairs." Maggie smiled warmly. "But it showed me that you have ingenuity and courage in a difficult situation. Those things added to your kindness, your sincerity, and your humor have given me a clear idea of your worth as a man."

It was high praise. But Eli knew his background and he knew who he really was.

He sighed, "Mrs. Blaine, I'm sorry to say, but I'm not all that good. I've been involved in considerable shecoonery[2] in my time."

She took another sip of tea and placed the cup back on the saucer. The china clinked almost musically as she did it.

"Well," she said, easily, "then let's just say, sir, that the past is the past. Anyway, who am I to cast stones? My point is you no longer will need to engage in such pursuits. Now that you live here and have a shop, that is."

"Ah," he said, not sure whether to believe her words.

Maggie's hazel eyes met his. "You do mean to stay, do you not, Mr. Smith?"

He did not reply. Because he didn't know. He never knew. He never really stayed anywhere these days. He had not done so for a long time.

"It all depends on what happens," he hedged.

Maggie tipped her head.

"You know. If the paper succeeds. And," he added with a grimace, "if no one burns it down."

"I understand. You have had quite a journey, haven't you?"

---

[2] Shecoonery is a corruption of chicanery.

"I suppose you could say that."

"No supposing about it. You left your home. Where was it, by the way?"

"Pennsylvania," he answered vaguely.

Maggie nodded. "So, you left Pennsylvania and went to New York City. Then you traveled west into the Sioux country. Then back to Ohio. And now you're here." She tipped her head again. "Do you intend to continue your journey to New York at some point?"

"I don't know." And Eli realized that he did not know.

"Well! I think it would be a pity if you ever left here, Mr. Smith. I'll pray that your newspaper flourishes."

"Thanks. Flourishing is kind of what I had in mind."

Maggie smiled. "That's good. Because..." She paused.

"Because what?"

"Because I think you're finally home."

Eli considered the idea. "Home, huh?"

She reached across the table and laid a hand over his. "Yes. Home."

Her hand was warm and welcoming.

"And," she continued, "you have friends here. Some very good ones."

"I do," he agreed.

"I would like you to stay."

Her words gave him a sense of comfort and security that he had not felt in a long time.

17 April 1855

And that was when Elijah Smith knew for a fact that his wandering days were over. He *was* home.

Finally.

About the Author

As Founder of Squeaking Pips, Janet wears many hats: author, editor, designer, and encourager of new authors. Born in Albany, New York, she spent most of her childhood and the bulk of her teen years in Parsippany, NJ. She attended Seton Hall University (South Orange, NJ) where she received a B.A. degree in Asian Studies. Some years later Janet attended Drew University, receiving a Master of Divinity degree and a Ph.D. in North American Religion and Culture.

Janet Stafford has served six congregations the United Methodist Church for over 25 years, working as an assistant pastor, director of faith formation and ministries with children, youth, and families, and more recently as communications director. She has been with her current congregation since 2008. She also worked as an adjunct professor at two universities where she taught interdisciplinary studies and history.

Through Squeaking Pips, Janet has published novels, novellas, and short stories, most of which follow the adventures of Maggie, her husband Eli, and their unconventional family as they navigate the challenges of Civil War-era America. Janet's other work, *Heart Soul & Rock'n'Roll*, is a

17 April 1855

contemporary romance set in her home state of New Jersey.

Other Books by Janet R. Stafford

Novels

Historical Fiction
Saint Maggie
Walk by Faith: Saint Maggie Series Book 2
A Time to Heal: Saint Maggie Series Book 3
Seeing the Elephant: Saint Maggie Series Book 4
A Good Community: Saint Maggie Series Book 5
Coming Soon: *Balm in Gilead: Saint Maggie Series Book 6*

Contemporary Romance
Heart Soul & Rock'n'Roll

Novellas

Historical Fiction
The Enlistment: A Frankie Blaine Story
The Great Central Fair: A Saint Maggie Story

Short Stories

Historical Fiction
"The Christmas Eve Visitor: A Saint Maggie Short Story"
"The Dundee Cake: A Saint Maggie Short Story"

www.ingramcontent.com/pod-product-compliance
Lightning Source LLC
Chambersburg PA
CBHW070649130626
46555CB00006B/2786